A Kitten
Named Tiger

Pet Rescue Adventures:

Max the Missing Puppy

Ginger the Stray Kitten

Buttons the Runaway Puppy

The Frightened Kitten

Jessie the Lonely Puppy

The Kitten Nobody Wanted

Harry the Homeless Puppy

Lost in the Snow

Leo All Alone

The Brave Kitten

The Secret Puppy

Sky the Unwanted Kitten

Misty the Abandoned Kitten

The Scruffy Puppy

The Lost Puppy

The Missing Kitten

The Secret Kitten

The Rescued Puppy

Sammy the Shy Kitten

The Tiniest Puppy

Alone in the Night

Lost in the Storm

Teddy in Trouble

A Home for Sandy

The Curious Kitten

The Abandoned Puppy

The Sad Puppy

The Homeless Kitten

The Stolen Kitten

The Forgotten Puppy

The Homesick Puppy

The Kidnapped Kitten

The Puppy Who Was Left Behind

The Seaside Puppy

The Rescued Kitten

Oscar's Lonely Christmas

The Unwanted Puppy

The Perfect Kitten

Also by Holly Webb:
Little Puppy Lost
The Snow Bear

A Kitten Named Tiger

by Holly Webb
Illustrated by Sophy Williams

tiger tales

tiger tales

5 River Road, Suite 128, Wilton, CT 06897
Published in the United States 2018
Originally published in Great Britain 2017
by the Little Tiger Group
Text copyright © 2017 Holly Webb
Illustrations copyright © 2017 Sophy Williams
ISBN-13: 978-1-68010-428-8
ISBN-10: 1-68010-428-4
Printed in China
STP/1800/0323/1219
10 9 8 7 6 5 4 3 2

For more insight and activities, visit us at www.tigertalesbooks.com

Contents

Chapter One
A Brave Kitten
7

Chapter Two
Exploring
24

Chapter Three
The Adventures Begin
38

Chapter Four
The Great Outdoors
51

Chapter Five
Tiger in Trouble
67

Chapter Six
A Disappearing Act
84

Chapter Seven
Stuck!
96

Chapter Eight
Ava's Brave Rescue
112

For Angel and Poppy—two adventurous cats!

Chapter One
A Brave Kitten

"Ava! Come on, wake up. Look at this!" Mom held up her phone in front of Ava's nose, and Ava squinted at the photo on the screen sleepily. Then she sat upright in bed and grabbed the phone. Ever since her parents had agreed to getting a kitten, Ava had been scanning the local animal rescue's website and checking the bulletin board in the supermarket. But no one seemed to have any kittens in need of homes—until now.

"Oh! They're beautiful! Mom, are they real? I mean, are they ready to be adopted? Can we go and see them?" The photo showed a litter of kittens snuggled up in a cardboard box—it wasn't a very big one, but they'd obviously all decided it was the best place to sleep ever. Ava was almost sure there were four in total, but it was difficult to properly count them....

8

"Yes, they're real, and yes, we can go and see them. Rose, the lady who owns them, put their picture online, and she said she's free this weekend if people want to visit. I've already sent her a message to see if we can go over today. Your Aunt Jen sent me their picture— Rose is a friend of hers. Aunt Jen said she thought of you as soon as she saw them!"

"They're so little and fluffy...," Ava cooed, petting the phone screen with her finger. Then she sighed as the picture disappeared. "Oops! Sorry, Mom, I'm still half asleep. I just wanted to pet them!"

Mom smiled as she took the phone back. "I love the orange and white one— but the striped kitten is adorable, too. I think we might have a really hard time choosing. Oh, look! Rose replied to my message, asking if we can come over at about 10 o'clock. Ooooh, I don't know, Ava. What do you think? It's a bit early for a Saturday, isn't it?"

Mom laughed as Ava leaped out of bed, flinging off the comforter. "You think we can, then? We have to get Sara and Erin up. And your dad is still asleep."

"We only have two hours!" Ava squeaked. "Wake him up now, Mom! And tell Sara and Erin we're going to see some kittens. They'll be out of bed the fastest you've ever seen, I promise!"

"Hurry up," Ava groaned. "There's the house, look, number 22. Sara, you don't need to bring your toy cat. We're going to see *real* kittens...."

"They will like my toy cat," her sister said firmly, gathering up her toy cat and her purse and all the cat's clothes, and clambering down from her car seat. Sara was only three—Mom and Dad had said they'd think about getting a family pet once she was old enough to understand that a kitten wasn't another toy for her to play with. Ava had been looking forward to Sara's birthday more than her own.

Ava's other sister, five-year-old Erin, had run ahead and was trying to undo the latch of the gate. She was just as excited as Ava was. Neither of them had been able to eat any breakfast, and they'd watched Dad and Sara plowing through their cereal with disbelief.

"Okay." Dad locked the car and led Sara over to the gate. "Let's go!"

Erin finally managed to unlatch the gate, and the front door opened as they walked up the front walkway. A lady in a striped T-shirt waved at them. "I saw you coming. I'm Rose." She scooped up a silvery tabby cat who was trying to escape around her legs. "And this is Muffin. She's the kittens' mom."

"She's beautiful," Ava's mom said.

"She really is," Rose agreed. "Come on in. Muffin is too young to have kittens, to be honest. She was a stray. She kept coming into the yard, and in the end I adopted her. I didn't know I was getting five cats instead of one!"

"Oh, wow…." Ava sighed. It sounded like a dream come true to her.

"Anyway, come and see the kittens. They're in the kitchen."

Ava could feel her heart thumping with excitement as they walked through the hallway. The kitchen door was closed and Rose opened it carefully, obviously trying not to bump into any kittens on the other side.

"Oh! Oh! A kitten!" Erin squealed as a little furry face popped around the edge of the door.

The kitten disappeared at once, and Mom shushed Erin gently. "Sweetheart, remember what we talked about. You have to be quiet around the kittens. If you shout, you'll scare them."

Erin nodded, but Ava could tell that she was so excited she wasn't really listening. Ava swallowed hard as Rose opened the door all the way. There seemed to be a bubble of nervousness stuck in the top of her throat. She had been daydreaming about this moment for so long!

The kittens seemed to have taken over Rose's kitchen. There were cat toys everywhere, a cozy basket sat next to the radiator, and a huge kitten jungle gym made of scratching posts and carpeted holes was squashed up next to the kitchen table. As they all went in, a small orange kitten looked up from licking the butter off a piece of toast.

Rose put Muffin down and sighed. "That was my breakfast," she told the kitten, lifting it off the table. "You've had yours." She looked at Ava and her family. "They're adorable, but they get everywhere." Then she frowned. "Hang on. How many kittens can you see?"

Ava laughed. Now that she could actually see the kittens, the strange feeling inside her had disappeared. "Three," she told Rose. "The one who was licking your toast...."

"There's another orange one over there on the jungle gym," Erin said.

"And there's a tabby kitten by the door," Ava added, peering around the table to get a better look. The tabby kitten was playing with a fluffy toy rabbit that was almost as big as it was, rolling over and over on the floor.

"There should be four," Rose said, scanning the kitchen. "We're missing one. There's another tabby kitten—and honestly, it's always him!"

Ava crouched down to check under the table, but there was only the orange kitten, still licking his buttery whiskers. Then, as she stood up, Ava spotted the tip of a striped tail on top of the bookcase. "Is that him?" she asked Rose, pointing. "Behind those photographs?"

"How did he get up there?" Dad laughed. "That's a huge jump for such a small cat."

Rose shook her head, smiling. "I didn't think any of them could get up there. But I suppose if he went from the jungle gym to the table, to the edge of the sink and then scrambled up the curtain.... This entire kitchen is like a playground for kittens. But he's definitely the most adventurous!"

"Hello," Ava whispered to the kitten as he eyed her around the side of the photo frame. "Are you stuck?" The kitten looked so funny with his head sticking out one end of the frame and his tail the other. He meowed at her and edged a little further out from behind the photo. But there wasn't much room, and he bumped into a vase that was standing behind him, making it wobble dangerously.

"Oh!" Ava said worriedly. "Come on, kitten. You're going to get squished in a minute." She reached up to lift him out from behind the picture frame, and then looked uncertainly at Rose. Was it okay to pick the kitten up?

Rose nodded at her. "Can you reach? Just lift him from there."

Ava slipped both hands around the kitten's middle, hoping she wasn't scaring him. But she thought he actually looked grateful to be rescued. He didn't wriggle at all, and she snuggled him against her cardigan, loving the feel of his warm fur and his squishy kitten tummy.

"Oh, he's very handsome!" Mom said, coming over to look. "So stripy!"

"He has the most stripes I've ever seen on a cat!" Ava agreed, looking down at the kitten. He was a beautiful golden brown color, with black stripes running down his sides and fat black rings all along his tail. Ava had seen tabby cats before, of course, but never one with such perfect stripes.

"He's what's called a mackerel tabby,"

Rose said. "Like the fish—they have stripes, too."

"He looks more like a tiger," Mom said. "The way his stripes match on both sides."

Ava giggled as the kitten scrambled up her cardigan and climbed onto her shoulder. She knew he was probably just trying to get up high, so that he could see what was going on with all these strange people in his kitchen, but it felt like he belonged with her somehow.

21

"Mom," she whispered. "Do you think…. Could we have this one?"

Sara stood up to see. She'd been trying to get the orange kittens to look at her toy cat, but they weren't very interested. "What's his name?" she asked Rose.

"Oh, well, I tried not to name them, because I knew they'd be going to new owners," Rose explained. "But in my head I've been calling him Adventure Kitten."

"He sounds like a superhero!" Ava said.

"I think his name is Tiger," Sara said, nodding her head. "Let's take him home now."

"Oh, Sara, we haven't decided yet," Mom said, but she was smiling. "And don't forget, we need to buy a cat carrier and a basket, and oh, lots of things! Although he *is* beautiful...."

"And Tiger would be a great name," Dad said. "Erin? Ava? What do you think?"

Erin reached up to pet the kitten's tiny paws and smiled. "Even his paws are striped."

Ava nodded, just a little, so as not to shake the kitten too much. "It's perfect! He looks just like a tiger, and he's as brave as one, too."

Chapter Two
Exploring

When the carrier was set down at last and the wire door swung open, Tiger didn't move. He wasn't sure what was outside the carrier, but he knew it wasn't his home. It smelled different. There was no comforting smell of his mother and the other kittens.

"Why isn't he coming out?" Erin said, crouching down.

"He's probably frightened," Mom explained. "This is all really strange for him."

"Should we try the cat treats? The ones Rose said he liked?" Ava suggested, opening the kitchen cupboard.

Tiger took a step closer to the open wire door as he heard the crinkle of the foil packet. He could smell the treats, too—the delicious fishy ones. Even though he was still scared, he padded forward another couple of steps and peered through the wire bars. Yes, there was the packet. His whiskers twitched, and he eyed the girl holding the treats.

"Come on, kitten!" Sara wriggled away from Mom and bounced toward the cat carrier. Tiger heard her voice and the thud of her footsteps and retreated back inside the carrier.

"Sara!" Ava snapped and then wished she hadn't when her little sister's face crumpled. "You have to be really gentle," she added, but Sara had already burst into tears.

"Maybe we should give Tiger some time to come out by himself," Dad suggested. "I know you all want to play with him, but he's nervous. Why don't we put on a movie?" He picked up Sara and led Erin out of the kitchen, but Ava hesitated. *She* could stay, right? Tiger liked her—he'd let her lift him off the bookshelf the day before, and he'd seemed happy for her to hold him then. She looked pleadingly at Dad, but he shook his head. "It isn't fair, Ava," he pointed out. "And there'll be plenty of time to play with him."

Mom put an arm around her shoulders. "We'll give Tiger time to explore a little by himself, then we'll all go and see how he's doing. Anyway, don't you have homework to do? How long should that take you—20 minutes? If you get it out of the way now, then you'll have the rest of the afternoon free to play with Tiger."

Ava nodded and sighed. Mom was right about the homework. But why did Sara and Erin always have to mess things up?

Tiger's ears twitched as the kitchen door clicked shut. He could still smell those cat treats. He crept to the carrier door and peered around it. There was a scattering of treats on the floor, and they smelled so good. He stepped out and then started to munch the treats, looking around carefully between each bite. But there were only a few, and they were gone in seconds. He looked uncertainly back to the carrier. He knew he was safe in there, but he didn't like it much. Now that the kitchen was quiet, he wanted to explore.

He jumped up onto a kitchen chair and then the table. He liked to be up high to see what was going on. He prowled across the table and eyed the window above the sink. The main window was mostly closed, but there was a smaller window at the top, and that was open. Just then, a bee looped in through the window from the yard. Tiger watched it with interest, not

really sure what it was. He crouched
down a little, wondering if he could
pounce on the bee from where he was.
It zigzagged around the kitchen, and
as it swooped back over the table he
followed it, his tail twitching with
excitement.

Tiger balanced at the very edge of the table, trying to swipe at the bee with his paw. But he just couldn't get close enough. Then the bee stopped for a rest, perched on the kitchen wall. Tiger hopped back onto the chair and down to the floor. He would creep up on it and pounce! Stealthily he padded across the tiles, and then he launched himself at the bee.

The bee flew away, buzzing frantically, and Tiger turned his head round to watch. He'd missed it by miles. Then he looked down and flexed his claws rather worriedly. They were firmly stuck in the thick wallpaper. He was halfway up the kitchen wall, and he wasn't quite sure how he'd gotten there....

Ava peered around the kitchen door, wondering where Tiger was. She had rushed through her homework—she was sure Mrs. Atkins wouldn't be impressed.

"I hope he's come out of the cat carrier," Mom said, looking over her shoulder. "But I can't see him. I'm surprised he's so shy—he seemed really daring at Rose's house. He was definitely the most adventurous of the four."

"Mom! Look!" Ava pointed across the kitchen at the wall, next to the fridge. Mom was always saying that she wanted to change the wallpaper, because she thought it was too bright and plastic-looking, but Ava liked it.

The paper was yellow, with a bright pattern of jam jars on it. Right now, though, halfway up there was a little striped kitten.

"How did he get up there?" Mom gasped.

"He must have climbed up," Ava giggled. "I guess the wallpaper is squishy enough that he can stick his claws in. Poor Tiger! Are you stuck? Can I get you down?" She walked slowly over to the wall. "How long have you been up there, silly boy? What did you do that for?"

"Just be careful, Ava," said Mom. "Don't pull at him; it might hurt his claws."

Ava put one hand under Tiger's bottom and tried to lift his front paws up a bit to unhook the claws.

"How is he?" Dad asked, putting his head around the door. "Settling in okay?"

Mom sighed. "You could say that. Look!"

Dad laughed. "Wow! That's one way to get rid of that wallpaper! Can you get him off there, Ava?"

"His claws are stuck right in," Ava said worriedly. "I can't lift his paws away, and he's so scared he's just holding on tightly. At least I've got him up now, so it's not like he's hanging there by his claws…. What are we going to do? Should we call Rose?"

Dad shook his head. "Just a minute. I've got an idea." He reached out and gently rubbed the top of Tiger's closest paw. The kitten looked at him, his ears laid back, and his eyes wide and anxious-looking.

"What are you trying to do, Dad?" Ava asked.

"My mom did this when our cat climbed the back of the couch and got stuck. Our old gray cat, Shadow—remember Grandma Shirley showed you his picture?"

Ava nodded. Her grandmother loved cats—she'd had several, and Ava had seen photos of all of them. Shadow was the beautiful gray, long-haired cat that Dad's family had owned when he was about Ava's age.

"It's working," Ava whispered as Tiger relaxed his claws and his paw came away from the wallpaper with a little popping noise. "Do the other paw, Dad!"

Dad rubbed Tiger's other front paw, and it happened even quicker this time. Tiger was free—his hind paws hadn't been stuck in quite as deeply. Ava lifted him away from the wall and put him down carefully on the floor.

The kitten stalked away, shaking his ears angrily, and Ava pressed her hand across her mouth, trying not to laugh. "I think he's embarrassed that he got stuck," she whispered to Dad. "He's pretending it didn't happen!"

"I hope his paws are okay," Mom said, leaning to the side to look more closely at how Tiger was walking. "He isn't limping, is he?"

"No, I think he's fine." Ava crouched down to check, and Tiger looked at her curiously. "Hey, Tiger. You're okay, aren't you? No sore paws?"

Tiger padded up to her and dabbed his nose against her knee.

Dad smiled. "Maybe that was a thank you."

Chapter Three
The Adventures Begin

"Mom, where's Tiger?" Ava dashed out into the yard, where her mom was planting some flowers. Ava's best friend Ella's dad worked as a gardener, and he'd given them to Mom at school the day before.

"Isn't he in the kitchen? He was asleep in his basket a few minutes ago. I think he was worn out after you girls waved that feather toy at him for so long." Mom stood up, taking off her gardening gloves.

"He's definitely not. I came down to check on him after I finished my math homework." Ava looked around the yard worriedly. "He didn't slip out after you, did he? He's not supposed to go outside yet!"

"I'm sure he didn't." Mom was silent for a moment. "I wonder where your sisters are…?"

Ava wheeled around and hurried back into the house. Sara and Erin had been in their room; she'd heard them giggling. But they knew Tiger was supposed to stay in the kitchen for the first few days! She bounded up the stairs and burst into their bedroom.

"Go away! We're busy!" Sara said angrily, but Erin looked nervous. She put a doll's blanket over something in front of her—something that was moving!

"You have Tiger up here!" Ava cried. "You know he's supposed to stay in the kitchen—we haven't even had him for a day!"

Tiger peered out from underneath the blanket, and Ava gasped. They'd been dressing him up. A doll's sock was falling off one of his front paws, and there was a hat balanced on one twitching ear.

Ava scooped him up and cuddled him against her. "You can't do that! He's not a toy!"

"How come you get to play with him and we don't?" Erin demanded. "We were just having fun. He's our kitten, too."

"You can play with him the right way, with cat toys! But you shouldn't dress him up like a doll." Ava slipped the sock off his paw—the hat had fallen off already.

"Give him back!" Sara whined.

Erin stamped her foot. "You're not taking him! It's not fair!"

"Oh, yes, she is," Mom said from the doorway. "You knew he wasn't allowed to come upstairs yet. And what's this about dressing him up? Please take

41

Tiger back to the kitchen, Ava. I need to talk to Erin and Sara."

Ava carried Tiger downstairs, petting him gently. "I bet you wish you could go back to Rose's house, where everybody was sensible," she whispered. "I can't believe my sisters were dressing you up. They were probably going to put you in the doll's stroller, weren't they?"

Tiger nuzzled under her chin. He hadn't liked Sara and Erin pulling him around, although he had been able to explore their room while they argued over which clothes to put on him, and that had been interesting. So many things to clamber around and sniff and investigate. But he liked Ava's calm, gentle voice, and the way she was petting his back over and over.

Ava sat down at the kitchen table, holding Tiger in her lap. She wasn't holding him tightly, and she was expecting him to leap down from her knee and go find somewhere to hide. Probably he'd want to disappear inside his basket—it was one of those soft furry igloo ones, so he had his own little cave to snuggle in. But he stayed, kneading up and down on her leg with his needle-sharp claws.

"It's a good thing I've got jeans on," she whispered to him. "Are you okay? You're not still scared?"

Tiger turned himself around slowly and then settled down into a little heap on her lap. He looked around and spotted his feather toy lying on the floor close to his basket. Maybe Ava would wave it for him some more? Then he slumped down again. No. He was too sleepy….

Ava watched him, a huge smile on her face. He was going to sleep—on her lap. Surely that meant he was happy, even after everything Sara and Erin had put him through.

Mom had explained to Erin and Sara again that Tiger was little and needed time to get used to all of them—and that kittens never, ever wanted to be dressed up. Ava wasn't totally sure that her little sisters understood, though. Sara definitely thought Tiger was a new and improved kind of teddy bear. Ava wasn't sure what to do—maybe Sara wasn't old enough for a pet, after all. But if she said that to Mom and Dad, they might agree with her and decide to take Tiger back!

"I'm going to tell Miss Daniels all about Tiger," Erin said, swinging her book bag around and around as she and Ava waited for Mom and Sara in the front yard. "And everybody in my class." She stopped suddenly. "I could take in Tiger for Show and Tell!"

"No!" Ava yelped.

"He wouldn't like it, Erin," Mom said, locking the front door. "He'd be scared. But you could take in a picture."

Erin was about to argue when she caught sight of one of her friends coming down the road with her mom and started waving. "Mia!"

Ava waved, too—her best friend, Ella, was Mia's older sister, and they all often ended up walking to school together.

"We have a new kitten!" Erin told Mia proudly.

Ella looked surprised. "Do you really?" she asked Ava. "I didn't know you'd found one!"

46

"We went to see a litter of kittens on Saturday and we brought him home yesterday. His name is Tiger."

"Oh, lucky you…," Ella sighed. "I love our cats, but they're both old and don't like to play very much. It'd be great to have a kitten to play with."

"You can come and play with Tiger," Ava said. "Oh, hi, Megan!" Ava smiled as their next-door neighbor came out of her gate and then crouched down to pet her dogs, Charlie and Max. "Are you going for a walk?" Ava loved the dogs. She sometimes went with Megan to walk them.

Charlie and Max wagged their feathery tails and yapped with excitement as all five girls doted on them—even Sara reached over from her stroller to pet their ears.

"We have a kitten," Erin told Megan.

"I wonder if Charlie and Max can smell that! They're very excited. Come on, you two. We're a little late this morning, so we only have time for a quick walk before I have to get to work," Megan told the girls. "Have a good day at school!"

"'Bye!" Ava and Ella led the way around the corner to the alley that went past the woods. It went almost all the way to their school and Sara's daycare. It was a little wild, with overgrown hedges and weeds growing up around the big trees, but because cars couldn't drive down there, it meant she and Ella could walk on ahead and their moms didn't mind.

"Oooh, look! Blackberries!" Ella reached into the bush to pick a couple and passed one to Ava. "So, is Tiger orange with stripes?"

"No, he's brown—golden brown, with really black stripes. And the tip of his tail is black, too, like he dipped it in a pot of paint."

"Awww.... Is he cuddly? I bet he's a bit shy still."

"He was when he arrived," Ava agreed. "But he loves playing so much, he forgets to be nervous around us. And he's really adventurous! When we first saw him at his old house, he was on top of a bookcase, and yesterday he climbed up the kitchen wallpaper and got stuck!"

Ella giggled. "He sounds like he's going to get into trouble!"

Ava nodded. "I know. I love it that he's so bouncy and full of energy, but I'm worried about what he might do next!"

Chapter Four
The Great Outdoors

"Look, Tiger." Ava put her hand through the cat flap and wiggled it around. Now that the kitten had had all of his vaccinations, he was allowed to go outside. Ava couldn't wait. She really wanted to see Tiger out in the yard for the first time. She was sure he was going to love having more space to explore.

Ella had been right about the kitten being trouble. Tiger already went everywhere in the house—and that meant *everywhere*. He seemed to be able to squeeze into the smallest space and scramble up the tallest piece of furniture. He'd even managed to jump from the bookcase in Ava's bedroom to the top of her bedroom door. Then he'd sat there, looking confused, as if he wasn't quite sure what he was supposed to do next. Dad had gotten him down, but Ava had a feeling it wouldn't be long before he tried again. Tiger just seemed to love being up high.

Ava let the cat flap bang shut again and looked at Tiger. He didn't seem to be getting it. He stared back at her.

He wasn't sure if this was some new sort
of game. Ava was good at
playing with him—
she would roll a
ball around for a
while, or bounce
his feather toy
up and down.
But now all she
seemed to want
to do was bang
at this strange hole
in the door.

Suddenly his ears pricked up and his
whiskers twitched. He had caught a
whiff of fresh air floating through the
cat flap. The scent of outside, where he
hadn't been allowed to go. He'd tried
to get out, of course, hovering behind

53

people as they went into the yard and sneaking after them, but they always caught him. He'd even gotten as far as the back step once, when Sara almost fell over and Mom was paying attention to her instead of watching the door. But then Mom had scooped him up while he was still staring out at the open stretch of grass.

"Come on, Tiger! You can go out," Ava told him, lifting the flap right up. "It's your own special door. Charlie and Max have one just like it, so they can get out while Megan's at work."

Tiger crept up to the cat flap and then jumped back as he saw Sara peering through it from the yard.

"When's he coming out?" she demanded.

"He was about to!" Ava said. "You scared him!"

Sara stomped away and Tiger poked his nose through the flap, looking out at the yard. It smelled so good, and he could hear birds scratching and fluttering in the bushes by the back door. He twitched his tail and hopped suddenly through the flap—so suddenly that Ava squeaked in surprise and had to scramble up and open the door to follow him.

"He's out," she called to Mom, who was pushing Erin on the swing. "Look at him!"

Tiger prowled along the patio, stopping every few steps to sniff at a leaf or watch an ant scurrying between his paws. Then he walked into a patch of bright autumn sunlight, feeling its warm glow on his fur. He sat down for a moment, closing his eyes and letting the warmth soak in. Then he lay down and rolled over, his paws in the air. He blinked lazily as a bee buzzed past but couldn't be bothered to leap up and chase it.

Mom laughed. "He looks completely relaxed."

"It's good, isn't it?" Ava said, sitting down next to Tiger. "And now you can go out whenever you like," she told him.

"Not for too long this first time, though," Mom said. "Remember what it said in the cat care book. We need to take him back inside for a snack, so he learns that it's a good thing to come back home. We don't want him to wander off and get lost. And we'll need to keep the cat flap locked when we're not around, at least to start with."

Ava nodded. "I don't think he's big enough to get out of the yard yet, though. Megan's walls are too high and there are no holes underneath, because she doesn't want Charlie and Max escaping. And there's the wall between our yard and the alley on the other side. Tiger's not big enough to jump onto that."

"I don't think it's going to be long," Mom replied. "He's such a good climber."

"I know." Ava sighed.

"This is really nice, Grandma." Ava nibbled a piece of popcorn and snuggled up next to Grandma Shirley. "We should do this more often!"

"Definitely," her grandma agreed. "We just have to persuade your mom and dad. It's very special for them to have a day out together."

"Shh!" Sara glared at them. "Don't talk!"

Ava and Grandma exchanged a look. Because Sara was the youngest, she seemed to think she had to be extra bossy.

"Where's Tiger?" Erin asked in a whisper. "I wanted him to sit on me while we watch the movie."

Ava smiled at her. "Do you want me to
go and get him? He's in his basket."

"Please!" Erin whispered back.
Grandma was smiling, too—she loved
Tiger. She'd told Ava she thought he was
the most adorable kitten she'd ever seen.

Ava hurried into the kitchen, but
there was no striped kitten in the basket.
She looked around the room—she even
checked the top of the door, just in case.
Tiger seemed to find places to hide

59

where she couldn't even imagine them. *He must have gone upstairs*, she thought, *or maybe he's out in the yard*. Now that he'd been allowed out for a few weeks, they left the cat flap unlocked in the daytime so he could go out by himself. She opened the back door and leaned out, calling, "Tiger! Tiger!"

She'd expected that he would leap out of the bushes by the back door. He loved lurking in there, watching the birds hopping around in the branches.

"Tiger!" Ava called again. But there was no answering meow, only Charlie and Max barking in the yard next door. *Barking a lot, actually*, Ava thought, wondering what was the matter. Megan worked on Saturdays in one of the department stores in town, so the dogs were on their own.

"Hey, Charlie! Hey, Max," she called over the wall. "Shh…. What's wrong?"

It was as if the dogs didn't even hear her. They just kept on barking.

Ava bit her lip, suddenly worried. She dashed back indoors and up the stairs, checking all the bedrooms to see if Tiger was curled up on someone's bed. But he wasn't. Ava leaned out of Sara and Erin's bedroom window, trying to look down into Megan's yard, but the wall was in the way. She could only see the back end of the yard, and she knew the dogs were near the house—she'd heard them close to the back door.

Ava dug her nails into her palms, trying to keep herself from panicking. She didn't know that Tiger was in the yard next door. How could he be? He wasn't big enough to get over that huge wall, and there were no gaps that he could have squeezed through. It couldn't be Tiger that Charlie and Max were barking at.

Ava wasn't completely sure, though. Not sure enough.

Tiger had been at the far end of the yard, stalking a blackbird. It had been brave enough to flutter down onto the grass right in front of him. The kitten had been so surprised that he almost fell over his own paws, but as soon as he realized what was happening, he sank into a hunting crouch. He had seen birds hopping around in the bushes before, but never one so close up. He inched forward, hardly breathing, creeping closer and closer. Then, all of a sudden, the bird spotted him and shot into the air with a frantic beating of wings. Tiger dived after it, but the bird was too fast. It was gone before he landed in the scrubby lilac bush that grew against the wall.

Tiger scrambled after the bird, and it squawked furiously at him and fluttered away over the wall.

He looked up as it flew off, with his ears laid back. He had been so close. Tiger clambered the rest of the way up the lilac bush, onto the wall, but the bird had disappeared. Then he gazed around curiously. He had never climbed onto the top of the wall before. He was high up enough to see all along the yard—and into the yard next door. A whole new place to explore!

He paced along the bricks, wondering if there were any other cats down there. A huge white cat had appeared in his own yard a couple of days before and hissed at him as though he wasn't meant to be there. He had been furious and scared all at the same time. But then Erin and Ava had come outside and started shouting, and the white cat had dashed away.

The new yard seemed very still, so he sprang down onto the grass and began to wander around, sniffing curiously at the plants. He was just investigating the tiny pond next to the patio when there was a sudden bang, followed by an ear-splitting series of barks.

Charlie and Max came shooting out of their dog flap, barking so loudly that Tiger just froze to the spot. He stood perched at the edge of the pond, trembling in fright and completely unable to move.

Tiger had seen the dogs before, out the window—he'd even heard Charlie and Max when he was in his own yard. But he hadn't known they lived here! He hadn't realized that this yard belonged to them.

Terrified, Tiger ran at last, racing toward the gate.

Chapter Five
Tiger in Trouble

"Ava, are you all right?" Grandma called up the stairs.

"I can't find Tiger!" she said, dashing down to Grandma. "And the dogs next door are barking like crazy. Do you think Tiger could have gotten into their yard?"

Grandma looked doubtful. "I doubt it … with that big wall? But then again, cats really are amazing climbers...."

"I know. I have to check, Grandma, but I can't see over the wall from the back windows. I've tried."

Ava hurried out into the yard and looked up at the wall helplessly. She'd never be able to see over it. It was more than six feet tall. Ava drew in a deep breath—the wall was just too big. Tiger couldn't have jumped on top of it, could he? But then, he'd managed to jump onto her bedroom door.... He might have managed it if he'd jumped onto something else first. She had to make sure.

"Grandma, can you please hold on to this chair for me?" Ava asked, pushing one of the lawn chairs up against the wall. "I need to look over the top."

She stepped up onto the chair. "Oh, no. It's no use—it's not tall enough." She was still a long way from being able to see into the yard next door.

"Oh, Ava, be careful," Grandma gasped as she jumped down. "I don't want to have to call your mom and dad and tell them I've had to take you to the hospital with a broken leg!"

"I am being careful, Grandma, I promise. But I have to see if Tiger is there...." Ava shuddered. "Charlie and Max are nice dogs, Grandma, but listen to them. They sound so fierce. Do you think you can help me push the table up against the wall? I can get on the chair, then the table, and then I think I'll be able to see over the top."

Grandma sighed. "I suppose there's not much else we can do. I'm so sorry, Ava, but I really don't think I can climb up there."

"I'll be fine, Grandma, honest. Here, just push this for me." Ava grabbed the edge of the metal table, dragging it toward the wall. "It's coming!" With Ava pulling and Grandma pushing, the table bumped up against the wall.

"Why are you in the yard?" Erin was standing at the back door, with Sara peering around her.

"Oh! Go back inside, you two,"

Grandma told her.

"What are you doing?" Erin's bottom lip stuck out. She was going to cry, Ava realized.

"They won't go back inside," Ava told Grandma. "Not without having a huge meltdown. We have to tell them what's going on." She turned to Sara and Erin. "The dogs are barking a lot, and I can't find Tiger. I think he might be in Megan's yard."

Erin stared at Ava, her eyes round with horror. "But they might eat him!"

"Tiger!" Sara wailed. "I want Tiger!"

"I do, too," Ava said, stepping up onto the chair. "So that's why I'm climbing up here. Now, you have to be good and not cry."

Grandma nodded. "Ava's right. Come

out here, you two. I know you only have your slippers on, but that's okay. You can help me hold the table so Ava doesn't wobble."

Sara and Erin padded out and held on tightly to the edge of the table. *It was clever of Grandma to get them to help*, Ava thought as she crawled cautiously up onto the table. Now they wouldn't whine about being left out.

"Is he there?" Sara gasped, as Ava balanced herself against the wall and stood up.

"I can't see yet." Ava peered over the top, looking anxiously around the yard. "Oh! Oh, Tiger!"

"He's there? Is he all right?" Grandma called up. "Oh, be careful, Ava! Hold on tight!"

"He's there, but I don't know if he's all right," Ava said, her voice shaking.

Tiger was curled up in a tiny ball, right by Megan's back gate. Charlie and Max were standing over him, still barking. The gate was a solid one, with no gaps in it and hardly any space underneath. And it was high, too. It looked like Tiger hadn't been able to scramble his way up and over—he was trapped.

"I don't think he's hurt," Ava called down. "Just really, really scared. But I can't tell for sure."

73

Max realized at last that someone else was invading his yard. He trotted over to the wall and barked at Ava.

Even though he was huddled up with his eyes closed, Tiger heard the difference in the barking. One of the dogs was gone! He opened his eyes a tiny bit and looked over.

Ava! She was there, looking over the wall! He tried to get up to run to her but the other dog leaned over him, barking even more fiercely, and Tiger huddled back down to the ground. He didn't dare move—he was frozen with fear.

"Oh, Tiger," Ava whispered. "Grandma, I have to get him out! He's so scared, and Charlie and Max might hurt him."

"What about the lady next door—when is she going to be back?" Grandma asked. "Do we have a phone number for her?"

"The home number is in Mom's address book, but that's no good. She's at work." Ava looked down at Grandma. "It'll be hours before she's back. Megan works until about six on Saturdays. I know she does because she told Mom she doesn't like it." Ava leaned over the wall again. "I'm coming to get you, Tiger. I'll be back in a minute."

"Coming to get him? No, you are not!" Grandma said, sounding horrified. "You can't get over there, Ava!"

"I'm not leaving him! Even if we call Mom and Dad, that food fair they went to is an hour away on the train. We can't leave him that long, Grandma. The dogs...." Ava's voice wobbled. "They're usually really friendly and nice, but you can hear how excited they are. What if he scratches one of them and they snap at him?"

Grandma stared at her uncertainly and then flinched as one of the dogs let out another loud bark. "All right. I suppose we do have to do something. But I don't see what, Ava. You can only just see over the wall—you can't get up there, and you certainly can't jump down on the other side. Then you'll be in the yard with those fierce dogs!"

"They aren't fierce, Grandma, honest. I see them almost every day with Megan, and I've even helped her take them for walks. They're barking because of Tiger, that's all."

"And how are you going to get back here again?"

Ava scrambled down from the table. "Dad's ladder. I should have thought of it before. It's in the shed. I can climb up onto the top of the wall, and then pull it up after me and put it down on the other side. It'll be fine, Grandma." Ava crossed her fingers hopefully behind her back. "I do stuff like this in gymnastics all the time."

"Things like throwing ladders around?" Grandma muttered. "Get the ladder, Ava, and let me see how stable it is. You won't have anyone to hold it on the other side. Oh, maybe I should have just called your mother…."

Ava threw open the shed door and grabbed the ladder. Luckily it was right by the door, and she didn't have to face the enormous spiders that lived in the shed. And it was lighter than it looked, too. She carried the ladder back to the yard and set it up by the wall.

Grandma, Sara, and Erin grabbed hold of it and Ava climbed up, trying to ignore the wobbling and creaking, and the thumping of her heart. "I'm going to climb on top of the wall now," she said,

refusing to let her voice shake. "And then can you help me pull up the ladder, Grandma?"

"Be careful," Erin called. "Please don't fall off, Ava!"

"I won't." Ava hugged the top of the wall and lifted her closest leg over so that she was sitting with one leg on either side. Just like the beam at gymnastics, except higher up, that was all.... She reached down and pulled the ladder up toward her, feeling grateful that it was so light.

"I'm coming, Tiger," she reassured him, looking over at the huddled pile of brown fur by the gate. "Don't be scared. It's going to be okay."

The dogs were very confused. They had a cat in their yard, and now somebody was climbing over the wall, too. They circled between Ava on the wall and Tiger by the gate, barking at both of them but wagging their tails at Ava—they knew her, even if she wasn't usually in their yard.

"Good dogs," Ava said, trying to sound calm. "Hi, Charlie. Good boy, Max. I'll be gone in a minute. I'm just coming to get Tiger. We'll both be out of here soon."

She rocked the ladder gently, trying to see if it was steady—but Megan's patio was gravel, not solid paving slabs like in her yard, and the ladder kept shifting. Ava gritted her teeth and climbed onto it anyway. She wasn't giving up now. It swayed and wobbled, and Ava closed her eyes and jumped. The ladder fell over with a crash, and there was a wail from the other side of the wall. Sara and Erin were crying.

"Ava! Ava! What happened?" Grandma called frantically. "Is everything okay?"

"I just jumped off the last part of the ladder. I'm fine, Grandma, I promise. Tell Sara and Erin I'm okay. Down, Charlie! Down, Max!" Ava hurried across the yard to the fence, the dogs getting under her feet as she ran.

"Poor Tiger!" She scooped him up and pressed her face against his soft coat. "Come on. We're getting out of here," she whispered to the little kitten. "I've got him, Grandma!" she called.

She dashed back to the ladder, pushing it close against the wall with her free hand. The dogs stood watching, occasionally wagging their tails. *They've probably never had such an exciting afternoon*, Ava thought.

Tiger wriggled a little, realizing that he was safely away from the dogs. He was with Ava. He was almost home! He didn't understand what had happened, but the terror that had gripped him as the dogs chased him across the yard slowly began to slip away.

Ava reached up and gently placed him on top of the wall. Tiger stood there for a moment, gazing down at the yard next door and the dogs. Then he looked back at Ava as she cautiously climbed the ladder.

"Are you going to be able to get back up?" Grandma called.

"I'm coming," Ava said as she reached the top of the ladder and pulled herself up onto the wall. "Oooh. Ow."

"Ava?" Erin cried anxiously.

"Don't worry. I just scratched my arms a little." Ava petted Tiger and waved down to Grandma and her sisters. "It's all okay!"

Chapter Six
A Disappearing Act

Tiger's adventure in the yard next door was going to become part of their family history, Ava realized. She told the story to Mom and Dad as soon as they got back. And then to Ella on the way to school on Monday, Mrs. Atkins during homeroom, and all her friends at recess. When Dad came home that night, he said he'd told everyone at work about her heroic rescue. Ava didn't feel very heroic, though. After she'd finally gotten back down the ladder, she'd suddenly started shaking. She never, ever wanted to go up one again.

Ava was pretty sure it wasn't going to be the last time they would have to rescue Tiger, either. But hopefully he wouldn't try getting into Charlie and Max's yard again, not after his huge scare.

The other good thing about Tiger's adventure was that it seemed to have made Erin and Sara understand that Tiger had to be taken care of and kept safe. Sara was a little too young to understand completely, but she was old enough to run and tell someone if she saw Tiger out in the front yard or on the wall between the yard and the alley. Ava felt like the three of them were a team.

Maybe it was because everyone was watching out for him so carefully, or maybe he was keeping to the safety of the house after having such a scare, but Tiger behaved beautifully all that week. He didn't get stuck anywhere. He was always around whenever anybody called for him. He didn't even sneak out into the front yard and worry Mom by gazing at the road.

But then on Sunday, exactly a week after his great escape, Tiger disappeared again.

Ava had been working on a project for school—it was due soon, so she spent all of Sunday afternoon drawing pictures of Mayan headdresses and copying chocolate recipes. She didn't notice that she hadn't seen Tiger. Erin had a birthday party to go to, and Sara was upset because she didn't. It wasn't until Dad started making dinner and got out the cat food to feed Tiger that everyone realized they had no idea where the kitten was.

"Ava? Is Tiger up there with you?" Dad called up the stairs.

Ava came out onto the landing. "No. I haven't seen him since lunchtime." She looked at her watch. "He hasn't come in for his dinner?"

Dad smiled up at her. "I'm sure he'll turn up in a minute. Don't worry, Ava."

Ava went back to her project, but she couldn't concentrate. After spending

10 minutes writing one sentence, she went downstairs. "Dad, is he back?"

"No," her dad admitted. "I went out in the yard and called, and I had a quick look around the front, too."

"Should I go and check again?"

"All right, but don't go far. It's getting dark."

Ava let herself out the front door and started to walk along the pavement, calling to Tiger. She hoped that any moment she'd see a little striped cat racing along the road toward her.

"Ava, what are you doing out here?" Mom and Erin had pulled up in the car outside the house, and Ava hurried over to them.

"We can't find Tiger! Mom, should I ring Megan's doorbell? Just to see if he's in her yard again."

"Let's do that," Mom replied, following Ava up their neighbor's front walkway, with Erin clinging to her hand.

Megan answered the door right away, smiling until she noticed Ava's anxious face. "What's wrong, Ava? Oh, no, the dogs haven't chased Tiger again, have they?" She looked down at Max and Charlie, who were bouncing around by her feet.

Ava had told Megan all about the rescue mission—Mom had taken her over the following day to apologize for climbing over the wall. Megan had said it was an emergency, and that she would have done exactly the same thing. She said Ava was very brave, and she'd given Mom a spare key to the gate in case it happened again.

"We can't find him!" Ava gasped. "Tiger's always back for dinner, always!"

"Megan, could you please take a quick look in your yard?" Mom asked.

"Of course. Here, you two, in here, come on." Megan shut the dogs into her living room. "I'll just go and see. Hold on a minute."

Ava waited, breathing fast. She wasn't sure what she wanted Megan to say. If the dogs had chased Tiger again, he would be so scared. But if he wasn't in her yard, it meant that they had no idea where he was....

Tiger had jumped onto the wall between the yard and the alley. It was a jump that he'd only just gotten big enough to do—he had to leap onto the back of the yard bench and then up onto the wall, and it was a tough scramble. But once he was up there, he could walk along it all the way down the side of the house to the front yard and the street. Then he could sit on the wall and watch people and cars going past, or even jump down onto the pavement. There were all sorts of interesting smells out there and a tree in the yard next door that was always full of sparrows. Tiger had never caught a bird—but of course he was going to keep trying.

That afternoon, the sparrows were particularly loud, and they kept fluttering around in the bush outside Megan's house in a very interesting way. Tiger hopped from Ava's front wall down onto Megan's and prowled along to be closer to the tree. But he wasn't quick enough, or quiet enough. The sparrows heard the little thump as he dropped down and they flew away, scolding shrilly.

Tiger stood on the wall, staring at the empty bush. Then he simply pretended that he hadn't been trying to chase the sparrows at all and leaped down onto the sidewalk.

He stalked along angrily, wondering if he could figure out where the sparrows had fluttered away to. He was thinking about the birds and not paying that much attention to anything else.

"Hey!" All of a sudden, there was a strange hissing noise behind him, followed by a squeal and an angry shout. Tiger darted out of the way with a yowl of fright as a bike skimmed past him. The rider's leg brushed against the kitten, shoving him sideways. Tiger shot away down the sidewalk, but he was so scared that he ran right past his house and into the alley. He'd never been down the alley before, but he didn't care. He just wanted to get away from the bike and the angry rider.

Tiger dashed along the alley, but it didn't feel far enough. He had to go up. If he was up high, he would be safe. No one would be able to catch him. He leaped and scrambled up into one of the tall trees. Still shaking from fright, Tiger kept climbing, higher and higher. He had to get as far up as he possibly could.

At last he stopped, crouched on a branch right at the top of the tree. Trembling all over, he gazed out into the darkening night.

Chapter Seven
Stuck!

"No one's seen him at all?" Dad asked as Mom and Ava came back in. He'd been putting Sara and Erin to bed while Mom and Ava went out searching for Tiger.

"No. But it's 8 o'clock. Ava needs to go to bed."

"I don't want to!" Ava protested. "Honestly, Mom, there's no way I could sleep now when we still don't know where Tiger is."

"You've got school tomorrow. No, Ava, I'm not arguing. It's bedtime. I promise Dad and I will keep looking up and down the street. We'll take turns. And we've asked all the neighbors, too. If anyone sees Tiger, they'll call us."

"He hasn't been missing that long," Dad pointed out. "Only a few hours, since after lunch sometime."

"Dad! He never, ever misses dinner!" Ava pressed her hands to her eyes. She'd been trying really hard not to cry—she knew it wouldn't help—but she was so tired and scared. And if *she* was scared in her warm, safe house, how was Tiger feeling? What if he was lost or hurt?

"I know some cats stay away for a long time," she went on, her voice shaking. "But Tiger doesn't. He's still little, and he loves home! He does silly things, but he doesn't go far away. He might be trapped somewhere. Or maybe he's been hit by a car!" She couldn't hold back her tears anymore.

Mom pulled her into a hug. "Ava, sweetie, I know you're scared. But it's too soon to panic like this. Dad's right. Tiger will probably pop through the cat flap in an hour or so, looking like he's never been away.

And you can't stay up any longer. Come on. It's time for bed."

Mom shooed Ava up the stairs and she went to her room, dragging her feet all the way. She couldn't imagine that she'd ever sleep. She was much too worried. She put on her pajamas and trailed into the bathroom to brush her teeth, all the while straining her ears for the bang of the cat flap. It didn't come. She climbed into bed and lay there, crying silently into her pillow.

"Ava! Ava!"

I must have fallen asleep, Ava realized. If she hadn't, no one would need to be waking her up....

That was Erin, Ava thought sleepily. And there seemed to be something heavy weighing down her feet. She sat up, blinking. Her room was still dark but she could see, just a little, by the nightlight on the landing. "What's the matter? It's not time to get up...," she whispered.

"We're worried," Erin told her.

The strange heavy lump on Ava's feet turned out to be Sara, sitting on the end of the bed. "Worried...," she echoed.

"About Tiger?" Ava sighed. "Me, too."

"You have to find him, Ava," Erin said seriously. "You rescued him from Charlie and Max. You climbed over the wall! I want him back. And so does Sara."

"We'll look for him again tomorrow before school," Ava said, trying to sound confident. "I bet we'll find him."

"Do you *promise*?" Erin demanded.

"Um." Ava swallowed hard. How could she promise? But Erin and Sara looked so scared. "I promise...," she whispered.

Tiger stretched and shivered. He was so cold, he ached. He had spent the night huddled up on his branch, sleeping every so often but then being shocked awake as he remembered the bike almost running him over.

He desperately wanted to go back home to Ava and his family, and have them pet him and snuggle up with him and make him feel safe. But he didn't dare go back down the tree, even though he felt so terribly hungry. It was starting to get light now—it felt like breakfast time, except that he'd missed his dinner, so his stomach was doubly empty. He needed a drink, too....

Tiger gazed down through the early morning mist. He could just make out the road from up here. The occasional car zoomed past, making him shrink back against the tree trunk, but they never came anywhere close. And there was no sign of the man on the bike. Maybe it was safe to climb down now....

Tiger stood up cautiously. The cold seemed to have made it harder to know what he was doing—his paws didn't feel quite right, and he shook as he tried to walk along the branch. He dug in his claws and hung on, suddenly feeling the wind blowing through the tree and shaking the branches. Until now he had felt safe up in the tree, so far from everything else. He hadn't thought about getting down.

He had gone up the tree so fast, he hadn't really thought about anything at all, only escaping. Now that it was light and he could see the ground, it seemed so far away from him, and he realized that he was higher up than he had ever been before. Much higher up than he wanted to be. Tiger meowed in sudden fright, again and again. He was stuck.

Ava ran out of school, still pulling on her raincoat, with Ella chasing after her. She had spent the entire day watching the hands creeping around the classroom clock, desperate for dismissal, so she could go and search for Tiger again. Mom had promised that if he turned up, she would call the office and ask the school secretary, Mrs. Marshall, to take a message down to Ava and Erin saying that Tiger was back. There hadn't been a message, though. Ava had even gone to the office at lunchtime to check, just in case Mrs. Marshall had been too busy to come to her class.

Mom had also explained to her teacher, Mrs. Atkins, which was good. Otherwise, Ava thought she'd probably have gotten into trouble, as she'd hardly done any work all day. She'd just been waiting and waiting.

She could see Mom and Sara by the gate, but Mom didn't look happy—she'd probably be jumping up and down and waving if it was good news.

"Did you ask the neighbors again?" Ava burst out, looking up at Mom anxiously.

"I did. Sara and I went all the way up and down the street, and to the roads close by. And I called the vet, but they hadn't seen him, either. That's good news, Ava. It means—" Mom swallowed—"well, it means he hasn't been hit by a car and was taken there."

Ava nodded, her eyes filling with tears again. She sniffed. "Yes. That's good."

Ella came hurrying up and gave Ava a hug. "We can look for him on the way home. I really want to help and my mom will, too. Mia is going over to play with Erin."

Ava's mom smiled at her. "Thanks, Ella. I'm sorry we didn't walk with you this morning. We were so late that I ended up taking the girls to school in the car—we went looking for Tiger again before breakfast." She sighed. "Not that you ate anything, Ava. Please tell me you ate your lunch? Dad told me you didn't have dinner last night, either."

"I ate a little," Ava said. She had—a

tiny bit. She just didn't feel hungry. There was too much worry inside her to fit in food, too.

"There's Erin." Mom waved as Erin's class came out onto the playground. Ava went over to the gate and stood a little ways away with Ella. She didn't want to hear Mom explaining to Erin that Tiger was still missing. She'd tried so hard to be brave and to tell Sara and Erin that it was going to be okay —but she was starting to think that it wasn't going to be okay at all.

Tiger had watched people going along the sidewalk all day long. He'd meowed, hoping they'd look up and

🐾 Stuck! 🐾

see him and help him get down. But it was a wet, windy day, and the few people hurrying by hadn't heard the sad little noises up above. He was starting to feel desperate. Every time the wind gusted the tree shook, and the branch where he was perched swung up and down.

Where was Ava? Why had he gone out into the front yard in the first place? He should have just stayed safe at home with Ava and Sara and Erin!

There were footsteps again now. But no one was going to hear him—they hadn't all the other times. Miserably, he slunk back along the branch, right up against the trunk of the tree, trying to stay out of the wind.

The footsteps came closer—they

109

were almost under the tree now. And then Tiger's ears pricked up as he heard a familiar voice.

"I'm sorry, Ella. I'm just so worried about him. If I cry in front of Erin and Sara, they'll be really upset. They think that because I rescued Tiger before, I'm going to be able to find him."

"We *will* find him," Ella said, giving

Ava a quick hug. "I'll help you make some posters when we get back. He's probably stuck in someone's shed."

"Maybe…."

Tiger sprang up, forgetting for a moment that he was scared of the swaying branch. He darted out as far as he could and meowed frantically for Ava.

Chapter Eight
Ava's Brave Rescue

Ava froze in the middle of the sidewalk. "I heard him! Ella, I heard Tiger meowing!"

Ella stopped, staring around. "Oh, wow! I heard him that time, too! Where is he, though? I can't see him."

Ava turned around slowly, listening for the meowing, trying to figure out where it was coming from. She was almost certain it was Tiger—he was all right! At least she hoped he was. He sounded scared.

"I can't see him. Oh! Ella, look! He's up there!" Ava pointed over to the tall tree by the side of the alley.

"Where?" Ella squinted up at the tree. "Are you sure?"

"Yes!" Ava's voice shook. She pointed again, impossibly far up into the branches. "Right at the top. Tiger! Tiger! He can see us!"

Tiger yowled loudly and started pacing up and down the branch.

Ella swallowed. "Do you think he's been there all this time? Is he stuck?"

"He must be. Mom! We found him!" Ava waved madly at her mom, who was just catching up with them, along with

Ella's mom. "Erin, he's here!"

Erin ran over, and Mom broke into a jog with Sara's stroller. "Up in the tree? I should have known he'd be stuck somewhere silly! Oh, Ava, I'm so relieved. Great job...." Her voice trailed off as she looked up into the tree and saw how high up Tiger was. He was still walking up and down the branch, meowing down at them. "Oh my goodness!"

"How are we going to get him down?" Ava asked, clutching her mom's arm. "I don't mind climbing trees, but I don't think I can get up that far."

Mom shook her head firmly. "You're definitely not climbing. I don't want you stuck up there, too. We could call Dad, but it'll take him a while to get back from work. I wonder if we could call the fire department."

"A fire truck?" Erin asked, hopping up and down excitedly.

"They couldn't get a fire truck down here," Ella's mom put in. "But Dave might be able to reach her if he used his long ladder."

Ava looked at her hopefully. Dave was Ella's dad, and he had ladders for trimming trees. "Does he have a really

115

tall ladder? We only have a little one."

Ella's mom nodded, smiling at her. "He definitely does. And I'm pretty sure he said he was doing a yard down the road today. It's going to be all right, Ava." She pulled her phone out of her pocket. "Hey, honey. Are you almost done? You're on Fairfield Road, aren't you? It's Ava and Erin's kitten. He's stuck up a tree in the alley by their house. Do you have your long ladder with you?" She listened for a moment and then said, "Thank you so much! See you in a minute." Then she patted Ava's shoulder. "It's okay. He was just finishing up. He'll be here soon."

Tiger peered down through the branches at Ava. He wanted to get to her so badly, but he didn't see how he could. Ava kept calling up to him. He loved hearing the sound of her voice. Surely she'd find a way to bring him down!

Then he saw someone else—a man carrying a long ladder. Ava and the others rushed over to talk to him, and Tiger stared at them, wondering what was happening. Then the tree shook a little as the ladder was pushed against it, and Tiger gave a little meow of fright as he felt the branch shake again.

Tiger sank his claws tightly into the bark. The ladder was growing taller now, pushing up toward him.

Tiger was still jumpy from the incident with the bike and an entire night stuck up the tree on his own, and he hated the look of the metal thing that was getting closer and closer. What was going on? Why wasn't Ava coming for him?

Meowing, he started to edge back, out along the branch to the narrow end, shaking and bouncing in the wind. He had to get away before that metal thing reached him.

Ella's dad climbed back down the ladder, shaking his head. "It's no good. He's terrified, poor little thing. He's going further and further along the branch as I get closer to him. I don't want to risk it."

Ava's mom sighed. "Oh, no. Thanks so much, Dave. Maybe I should try? He might be okay with someone he knows."

"Mom!" Ava stared at her. "You can't! You hate heights." Dad was always teasing Mom about it. She didn't even like the big slide at the amusement park. "What about me?" Ava asked, swallowing her nerves. She really didn't want to climb another ladder—not after she'd almost fallen off that ladder a few weeks ago. But someone had to get Tiger down.

Mom shook her head. "I don't want you going up that high! And how are you going to climb down again with a wriggly little kitten?"

"Tiger isn't wriggly when Ava carries him," Erin put in.

Ava nodded. "I've got a better idea, anyway. Why don't we get the cat carrier? If I put that on the branch, with cat treats in it, he'd definitely climb in. Then I could shut the door and pass it down to Ella's dad."

"That's actually a really good plan," Dave agreed. "I could climb up behind Ava and help her. The ladder's not strong enough for two adults on it at the same time, but Ava and I should be fine."

Mom nodded slowly. "All right, if you think that will work. I'll run home and get the carrier and the cat treats."

It seemed like the longest five minutes ever. Ava held Erin's hand, and they all took turns calling lovingly up to Tiger. But then, at last, Ava saw her mom come hurrying back.

"Okay, Ava," Dave said, as Mom opened the treats and placed them inside the carrier. "You start climbing up. Your mom and Ella's mom are going to hold the ladder steady, and I'm going to climb up behind you with the carrier. I'll pass it to you when you're ready."

Ava nodded, trying to wriggle her

fingers. They felt so cold, and she knew it was only because she was nervous…. But what if she slipped while she was climbing the ladder? It was at least twice as high as the wall that separated the yards.

She just couldn't slip. It was simple. She had to do it.

Slowly, she put her foot on the first rung of the ladder and began to climb. She didn't look down at the ground or even up at Tiger. She just looked at the rungs in front of her and kept going.

"I'm coming up behind you now, Ava. Hold on tight, and don't worry if you feel the ladder shaking!" Ella's dad called.

"Okay!" Ava called back, her voice odd and high. The ladder *was* shaking, and it was making her feel a bit sick.

"Ava, you're almost there!" That was Erin's voice, sounding a very long way below.

"A couple more rungs, Ava," Mom called. "You're doing so well."

Ava lifted her face a little to look up at the branches and gasped as she saw Tiger for the first time since she'd started climbing. He was there, staring at her, and he looked so scared.

Suddenly, Ava felt a tiny bit better. "Hey, Tiger," she whispered. "We're going to get you down." Carefully she went up two more rungs, so that she was right next to Tiger's branch. *I definitely wouldn't have been able to carry you back down*, she thought, shivering a little.

"Here's the carrier," Ella's dad said quietly. "Can you grab it? You'll have to let go with one hand. Take your time."

Ava nodded and forced herself to loosen her fingers and reach down. She grabbed the handle and shakily pushed the carrier up onto the branch. There was a forked piece of branch sticking out, and she wedged the carrier in it. Now she didn't have to hold on to it—otherwise, she'd have to let go with both hands to open the door. The packet of cat treats was inside—Tiger's favorite flavor, she noticed, the fishy ones. Ava reached in and shook the foil bag.

"How are you doing?" Ella's dad called up.

"He's coming!" Ava cried.

Tiger had started edging back along the branch. It was going to work! His soft fur brushed against her arm as he climbed into the carrier, sniffing at the bag. Ava shut the door so quickly she almost caught his tail, and then she secured the latch.

"He's in!"

"Terrific! Pass him down to me. Take it slow, Ava. The carrier is going to be heavy now."

Ava nodded, lifting the carrier and

reaching down to pass it to Ella's dad. She heard a worried little meow as the carrier moved. "It's okay, Tiger. We're going home," she whispered to him.

"Back down now, Ava. Nice and slow."

Ava wasn't sure how she ever got back down the ladder. She didn't even remember doing it. She was just there at the bottom, with Mom hugging her and saying she'd been so scared and she should never have let Ava go up there, and Erin telling her she was the best big sister ever, and Sara moaning because no one was listening and she'd dropped her toy cat.

Ava crouched down in front of the basket and peered in at the little striped face looking out at her.

"Please don't ever do that again," she whispered to Tiger. "Thank you so much for rescuing him," she told Ella's dad.

He grinned at her. "I didn't, Ava! It was all you! I think you'd better take him home and give him a lot of attention."

Ava nodded, picking up the carrier—she didn't even hold it by the handle; instead, she wrapped her arms around it, like she never wanted to let Tiger go. She could feel the kitten padding around inside as she carried him down the sidewalk and around the corner to her house. She said good-bye to Ella—she couldn't wave because she was holding on too tight to Tiger in his carrier.

Sara and Erin followed Ava into the house and crouched down next to her as she put the carrier down on the hallway floor. Tiger peered out at them, his ears twitching.

"It's all right," Ava whispered. "You're home now."

Tiger stepped slowly out of the carrier and then scrambled up onto Ava's knees, purring at last. She had come and rescued him. He'd known she would.